MATT CHRISTOPHER

On the Court with . . .

Grant Hill

MATT CHRISTOPHER

On the Court with . . .

Grant Hill

Little, Brown and Company

Boston   New York   Toronto   London

First Edition

Cover photograph by John McDonough, Sports Illustrated/© Time Inc.

Library of Congress Cataloging-in-Publication Data
Christopher, Matt.
    Grant Hill : on the court with — / Matt Christopher. —1st ed.
    p. cm.
    Summary: A biography of the son of former Dallas Cowboys halfback Calvin Hill who grew up to become a star basketball player with the Detroit Pistons.
    ISBN 0-316-13790-1 (pbk.)
    1. Hill, Grant — Juvenile literature. 2. Basketball players — United States — Biography — Juvenile literature. [1. Hill, Grant. 2. Basketball players. 3. Afro-Americans — Biography.] I. Title.
GV884.H55C57   1996
796.323′092 — dc20   96–22360

10 9 8 7 6 5 4 3 2 1

MV-NY

Published simultaneously in Canada
by Little, Brown and Company (Canada) Limited

Printed in the United States of America

To my wife, Cay

Contents

MATT CHRISTOPHER

On the Court with . . .

Chapter One:
1972–1986

Calvin Hill's Son

Grant Henry Hill was born in Dallas, Texas, on October 5, 1972. His father, Calvin Hill, was a Yale University graduate and a Dallas Cowboys running back; his mother, Janet Grant Hill, was a former Wellesley College roommate of first lady Hillary Rodham Clinton. They didn't call him Grant right away. Stumped for a name for their only child, they called him Baby Boy Hill until their good friend Roger Staubach, the Dallas Cowboys quarterback, suggested Grant (Janet's maiden name) and Henry (Calvin's father's name).

Grant grew fast — so fast that one doctor suggested he would be bowlegged unless his legs were broken and reset to straighten them. His mother, a strong-willed woman Grant and his friends later called the General, refused to let her baby go through so much pain.

The Hills lived in Dallas for two years after Grant was born, then moved to Hawaii so Calvin could pursue a career with the fledgling World Football League.

Even as a young child, Grant was impressed with the beaches and volcanoes of the Hawaiian Islands. But the WFL went out of business after just two seasons, and Calvin signed with the National Football League's Washington Redskins. Five-year-old Grant and his parents were on the move again.

Calvin and Janet decided to live in Reston, Virginia, a suburb sixteen miles east of Washington, D.C., because of its combination of safety and ethnic diversity. It was important to them that Grant be exposed to all different types of people so that he would learn to be considerate of others.

Grant's life growing up in Reston was a happy one. Both his parents had high-paying jobs — his mother worked as a consultant to the Pentagon — so money was never a problem. Their big house was filled with African paintings and sculpture, and plenty of toys. Grant learned to love music by playing first the bass guitar and later the piano. There were always lots of kids to play with in his neighborhood, and his school, Terraset Elementary, was a short walk away from the dead-end street his house was on.

"My world was literally that school and that dead end," Grant said in his autobiography, *Grant Hill: Change the Game.* "At that time, I thought it was the best place in the whole world."

Calvin and Janet Hill were able to give Grant all he needed, but he was far from spoiled. The General insisted that her son follow strict rules: he had to meet curfews, couldn't talk on the phone except for weekends, and wasn't allowed to go to parties or dances. But as exacting as she was, Janet also made sure Grant had fun. Once she took him and some friends to Disney World. The whole Hill family traveled to other places, too, like Egypt, England, and France.

Today, Grant credits his mother for helping him see that self-discipline, honesty, and hard work were important in achieving high academic and athletic standards. "She taught me to give it my best effort," Grant said, "and not to be satisfied unless it was my best."

From his father, Grant learned to love sports. He watched the Redskins practice and became a favorite of Joe Theismann and other famous Washington players. Grant enjoyed throwing and kicking a football around the yard with his dad every time he had the chance.

Yet the first organized sport Grant played was soccer. "My dad wouldn't let me play football when I was real young," he said. Pickup soccer games with the other kids in the neighborhood became a regular thing. In the summer, Grant attended soccer camp. By age nine he was a member of an all-star team from Reston that won the state championship and played in tournaments all over the East Coast. To this day, Grant credits soccer with developing his agility and explosive moves on the basketball court.

"That was really my first love," he said of the game.

When he was seven years old, Grant joined his first basketball team. Taller than all the other boys in the league, he was assigned the role of hanging by the basket and blocking shots. He found that assignment very frustrating because he felt he could move the ball just as well as any of the other players. His father understood his son's feelings; he advised him to dribble the ball upcourt after a rebound. Grant did, and from then on, he developed excellent ball-handling skills. By age eleven, he was playing for the local select team in competition with other all-star teams in Northern Virginia.

Grant worked hard to improve his game. He attended basketball camps in the summer and practiced his shooting, dribbling, and passing skills on homemade courts around his neighborhood.

Grant enjoyed watching basketball games almost as much as he did playing them. His mother took him to the hometown South Lakes High School games in Reston. His family had season tickets for the Georgetown University Hoyas, a perennial college power. A true student of the sport, Grant watched videotapes of basketball matches, then tried to duplicate in his own playing what he had seen. He was learning to think ahead, analyze each situation quickly, and react to plays intelligently and instinctively.

As he grew into his early teenage years, Grant took his game to the Twin Lakes Parks playground.

Frequently playing against older, more experienced boys such as Dennis Scott (currently with the NBA's Orlando Magic), Grant gained more confidence in his own ability.

Yet off the court, Grant's self-assurance all but vanished. At school, he was a shy, almost reclusive teenager. "I blended in with the lockers," he remembered, adding that his father's celebrity status was the main reason for this shyness. As the son of a famous football player, Grant figured people would try to be his friend because of who his father was. In fact, when his father once addressed his classmates, Grant pretended to be sick so he could be excused from the assembly. He just wanted to be his own person with his own identity.

It was on the court that he let people know who he was. In seventh grade, he hung up his soccer cleats to concentrate on basketball when he was chosen to play on a traveling Amateur Athletic Union team. The team's coach, Jim Warren, taught his players to outsmart their opponents. They learned to do that so well that Janet Hill nicknamed them "the Surgeons" for the way they dissected the other team's defense. During his eighth-grade year,

Grant's team won in the national AAU tournament in St. Louis, Missouri. They defeated teams that included future NBA stars Chris Webber, Jalen Rose, and David Robinson.

That victory was one of two significant events in Grant's pre–high school year. The second happened at the local playground. His father, who had recently retired from the NFL, challenged him to a game of one-on-one. Grant defeated the former All-Pro running back easily.

From then on, Calvin Hill chose to participate in his son's basketball career by watching games from the sidelines. And watch he did. He never yelled during the games, but afterward he would sit Grant down and go over them play by play. Grant called these sessions PGAs, or postgame analyses. Throughout his high school career, Grant Hill relived each mistake and missed opportunity of every game his father attended.

Such blow-by-blow replays were difficult for the teenager. He rebelled by pretending he didn't care about the sport he secretly dreamed of excelling at. When Calvin Hill had been playing pro ball, he had always readied himself mentally and physically for a game. Grant, however, could be found playing with a soccer ball, running around outside, or leaving for his game a mere hour and a half before it was to begin.

"Because he prepared so hard," Grant said later, "I wanted him to think that it came easy to me." Only when he was older did Grant realize how important pregame preparation was to how he played.

After two years of playing with the AAU team, Grant entered South Lakes High School. He was looking forward to playing on the freshman team with his boyhood friends. But South Lakes varsity coach Wendell Byrd had other plans.

Coach Byrd had scouted Grant closely for years. He was well aware of the freshman's talent, knowledge of the game, and superior work ethic. At six foot three, with good rebounding ability, Grant was penciled in to Byrd's varsity lineup.

Coach Byrd called Grant's father to explain the situation. He assured him that Grant had the ability to start for the varsity immediately.

But Grant resisted the idea. The last thing he wanted was to be in the spotlight. He just wanted to be one of the guys. At the same time, however, he was being given the chance to play with superior athletes a year or two earlier than he had expected. Going into his first year of high school, the shy thirteen-year-old had a tough decision to make.

Chapter Two:

1986-1990

Northern Virginia's Three-Time Player of the Year

In the end, Grant agreed to try out for the varsity team. To his relief, he was quickly accepted by his older teammates and had no problem playing at their level. As a freshman he played power forward, averaging 14 points and 7 rebounds a game.

The summer following his freshman year, Grant concentrated on improving his game even more. He worked out, continued to study videotapes, and played in pickup games at the Twin Lakes playground. The hard work paid off. At a fourteen-and-under national tournament in Seattle, Washington, he was voted Most Valuable Player.

Returning to the team the next year, the now six-foot-six sophomore exploded on the court. He led the South Lakes Seahawks to a 21–3 record, averaging 22 points and 10 rebounds a game. For his efforts, he was named the Northern Virginia Player of the Year.

As a junior Grant continued to play well. He broke the school's all-time scoring record. He helped lead South Lakes to the district playoffs. South Lakes went all the way to the final round. It was during this final playoff game that Grant Hill showed signs of the player he was to become later in his career.

South Lakes trailed by 10 points late in the second half. Jerome Scott, the senior captain and team leader, knew there was only one solution. "We need to get the ball to Grant," he said.

The Seahawks did just that. Grant scored the team's next 14 points, including 2 on an alley-oop dunk at the buzzer. He was again chosen Northern Virginia Player of the Year, as the Seahawks (27–2) won their first ever Northern Region title.

That summer, Grant was given the opportunity to play with some of the best young athletes in the country. He had been invited to participate in the exclusive Five-Star Basketball Camp, a three-week program that typically showcases the nation's best young basketball players. Michael Jordan had attended Five-Star when he was in high school, as had many other future NBA greats. For Grant Hill, the camp was an eye-opening experience.

After days of grueling but exciting play, Grant participated in the Five-Star All-Star game. At the end of the competition that typically features the best college prospects in the country, he was named MVP. Now standing at six foot seven, the sixteen-year-old had amazed the college scouts with his versatility. He seemed to be equally adept at forward or guard, handled the ball with finesse, and scored in the double digits consistently.

As he entered his final year of high school, Grant himself realized just how good he was. Even so, the flood of mail from colleges trying to woo him to their campuses was a little overwhelming. But he kept his head.

Throughout his life, Grant had been encouraged to take part in, but was never pushed into, sports. Academics always came first. He was an excellent student who exhibited a keen, inquiring mind. As his senior year at South Lakes High School progressed, he never lost sight of the importance of learning.

"I know this sounds funny," Grant told a reporter

for the *Sporting News,* "but it was almost like being born into a royal family and being raised like a prince being taught one day to become a king. Not just how to be an athlete, but how to do things right."

Grant Hill's dedication to academic excellence made him all the more attractive to colleges. And by the end of his senior year, he had unquestionably developed into one of the nation's elite players, listed among the top ten in the country.

Averaging 29 points, 11 rebounds, and 8 assists a game, he capped off his high school career with a banner season. He was named Northern Virginia Player of the Year for the third consecutive time and led South Lakes to a second appearance in the semifinals of the Virginia state high school tournament. Overall, the South Lakes Seahawks compiled a record of 25–4. Grant was chosen a *Parade* magazine high school All-American, the highest possible honor for a young basketball player.

"With ball handling skills that defy his size and a soft and accurate perimeter shot, Hill has become king of the hill in the northern region [of Virginia]," wrote Bobby Kaplow in the *Washington Post.*

His coach, Wendell Byrd, remembered him simply as "the premier player that people wanted."

Grant tried to take the attention in stride. As the son of a celebrity, he had learned a great deal from Calvin and his pro football friends about how to handle the media with class.

Still, the spring of 1990 became an especially hectic time for the Hill family. While they had little doubt that Grant would play basketball wherever he went, there was much more to consider than just a school's athletics program. Grant knew from his dad's experience that the road to becoming a professional athlete was an extremely difficult one. Calvin reminded him that the odds were slim for anyone to make it in professional sports. Even if he were successful, the average NBA career lasts just six years. The family knew the academic side of his decision would be vital.

With this in mind, Grant narrowed his options down to the schools he was most interested in attending: Georgetown, his mother's first choice, and North Carolina, his father's favorite, topped the list. Way down was Duke.

He visited Georgetown first. A discouraging interview was followed by a personally troubling realization: Georgetown was so close to his hometown that his parents would be able to attend almost every home game. That meant Calvin's PGAs would continue into college! Much as Grant loved his parents and the Hoyas' basketball program, another four years of such scrutiny seemed just intolerable enough for him to decide against Georgetown.

Next up was North Carolina. During the Hills' visit to the Tar Heels' campus, Dean Smith, the legendary coach of many all-time basketball greats including Michael Jordan, commented to Calvin that he was amazed by Grant's basketball knowledge. Thanks to the time off court with the VCR, Grant already knew most of the Tar Heels' plays!

Grant recognized that North Carolina had a lot to offer, but he wanted to be sure he had explored all possibilities before making his choice. His final decision surprised just about everyone.

"Duke? I hated Duke. I can't even tell you why I decided to visit there," he said of his alma mater. Yet after visiting the Durham, North Carolina, campus and talking with the basketball coach, Mike Krzyzewski, he knew where he belonged.

Many colleges routinely recruit players far too aggressively. Oftentimes promises are made and broken along the way. All of the other coaches who had recruited Grant were quick to guarantee an automatic starting position if he came to play at their school.

Coach K was different. He told Grant that the Blue Devils had a talented returning team. The freshman would have to earn his playing time.

Grant did not visit any other college after Duke. Krzyzewski had spoken to the competitor inside him.

"After learning a little bit more about Coach K and getting a better look at the school, I realized that Duke was definitely the place," Grant told the *Washington Post.*

The place that Grant Hill would spend the next four years has a longstanding reputation as one of the premier colleges in the country. A school of about 6,000 students, it has produced thirty-two NBA players. Most important to the Hill family, 94 percent of the Blue Devil players over the last twenty years have earned degrees. (Sadly, at most Division I colleges the graduation rate is just over 50 percent.)

Grant said, "That's one of the reasons why I picked Duke. I thought if I didn't play pro ball, a good education would set me up for something else."

Michael Ellison was as close to Grant as any of his friends growing up. He pointed out that it was important for Grant to make his own decision, and called it "Grant's independence day" when his friend chose Duke. He was referring in part to Grant's need to move out from under his father's shadow once and for all.

During the next four years, time would prove that there was no better fit for Grant Hill than Duke University. His development and exemplary performances on the court, in the classroom, and around campus would set a standard for all other student athletes to aspire to, not only at Duke but elsewhere in the country.

Chapter Three:
1990-1991

An Unbelievable First Season

Grant's last basketball competition before going to Duke was on a team of top U.S. high school athletes at the Junior Championship of the Americas in Montevideo, Uruguay. Grant and his team came home with a gold medal. He finished as the second-leading scorer with a 17.8 per game average and was named All-Tournament Player.

In the fall of 1990, Grant Hill moved to Durham, North Carolina. As the prize recruit at a basketball-crazy college, he was an instant celebrity. "The first day, there were people asking me for my autograph," he remembered. He longed for the opportunity to settle down and adjust to his new surroundings like any normal college freshman.

It was not to be. Even before he had played a game, the *College Basketball Yearbook*, a national publication that puts together lists of mock teams, selected him first team All-Freshman. Other publications had made him the consensus Atlantic Coast Conference Rookie of the Year.

All Grant wanted was to be ready to earn his place on Coach K's team. He knew he would be under careful scrutiny.

Mike Krzyzewski is one of the nation's most respected and honored college basketball coaches. In 1980, he arrived at Duke from West Point with instructions to get the sagging Blue Devils program back on track. He did just that, repeatedly leading his team to the National Collegiate Athletic Association's Final Four tournament year after year. The 1989–90 team had come closest yet to winning the national championship, though in the end they suffered a crushing defeat at the hands of the University of Nevada–Las Vegas.

When Grant Hill took to the court, he was joined by the dynamic duo that had led the team to the Final Four the year before: sophomore point guard Bobby Hurley and junior center Christian Laettner. "My very first day of pickup there, I got dunked on by Christian Laettner," Grant recalled. "I went back to the dorm, called my dad, and said, 'I don't know if I'm good enough to be at this level.' "

His father reassured him that he was. Coach Krzyzewski couldn't have been more pleased with the potential he saw in Grant. Here was a six-foot-seven player who had quickness, great leaping ability, and a good shooting touch from the outside. Grant's versatility allowed him to play any position on the floor: point guard, shooting guard, small forward, power forward, or even center if necessary. Grant appeared to be truly a unique talent.

Grant was one of five freshman recruits as the 1990–91 preseason practices began. The upperclassmen let the new kids know that the embarrassing 30-point loss of the previous year's NCAA championship was not to happen again. They were on a mission to get back to the Final Four and another opportunity to win the national championship.

During the preseason, Coach Krzyzewski became more impressed with Grant's all-around ability. "He has a special mind for the game," Coach K said. "There's not an aspect of the game he doesn't do well. He can play point guard, he can play inside, and he's a good passer."

After a month of rigorous practice, the Blue Devils were ready to open the season on their home court, legendary Cameron Indoor Stadium.

On November 14 in a preseason National Invitation Tournament (NIT) game against Marquette, Grant Hill, the latest Blue Devil sensation, made his collegiate debut before a sellout crowd. He played all five positions, dazzling the audience with his inside moves and accurate shooting. When substituted for point guard Bobby Hurley, he proved he could run the offense. He finished the game with 12 points, helping Duke pocket an easy 87–74 win.

In the second game of the season, Duke routed Big East Conference member Boston College, 100–74. The always difficult to please Coach K couldn't help commenting on the team's early-season commitment to his disciplined man-to-man defensive style. "I didn't expect us to be this good defensively this early in the season," he said. "I'm excited about our defense."

The next game for the Blue Devils was part of the NIT and scheduled to be played at the world's most famous gym: New York's Madison Square Garden.

Although Grant was settling in as a starter at forward along with senior cocaptain Greg Koubek, he was jittery before his first appearance in the Big Apple.

Other members of the team seemed to share Grant's nervousness. The Blue Devils' opponent, Arkansas, had been a tough competitor the year before and proved to be just as tough in this matchup. The usually reliable Hurley and forwards Koubek and Brian Davis hit only 4 buckets for 22 shots combined; Hurley turned the ball over a shocking 7 times. Despite a solid overall game by Grant (15 points, 6 rebounds, and 3 assists), the Razorbacks came out on top with a 98–88 victory.

Duke recovered to beat Notre Dame in the final round of the NIT in New York and went on to win a pair of games at home over East Carolina and UNC–Charlotte. Through six games Grant scored 10 or more points, the first Duke freshman since Johnny Dawkins in 1982–83 to do so. Consistency was quickly becoming Grant's trademark.

An early December loss to Big East powerhouse Georgetown at the Capital Center in Landover, Maryland, was particularly disappointing to Grant.

The game was the first he had played on the court where he and his parents had watched the Hoyas.

But that loss was the last for a while. Two solid wins over Big Ten team Michigan and Big Eight team Oklahoma highlighted a five-game winning streak that carried the Blue Devils through December into early January. With a half-season record of 10–2, the team was in good position for the Atlantic Coast Conference.

Off the court, Grant had adjusted to life at Duke. Initially undecided on which subject should be his major, he eventually chose history. It was the same choice his father had made at Yale a quarter-century earlier. Grant thought history would be useful, considering his interests in law school or teaching. Ever mindful that a professional sports career was a risky proposition, the Duke freshman wanted to make certain he would be well prepared for alternative careers.

As for living away from home for the first time, Grant was still very much an eighteen-year-old kid. At one point during his first semester he lost his room key. Too embarrassed to ask for a replacement, he pretended to lock and unlock his door for a whole month! His dorm phone was disconnected because he forgot to pay the bill.

On a more positive note, the other students in his dorm treated him the same as everyone else. That fact was more important to him than anything. The developing friendships with his teammates, especially roommate Antonio Lang, were also making his early college experiences memorable and satisfying.

At the start of the second half of the season, 8th-ranked Duke was ready for its first ACC test, a road game at the 18th-ranked University of Virginia in Charlottesville. But the fired-up Cavaliers dominated the Blue Devils from the outset. An 8-point halftime lead was extended to 19 in the second half. Duke turned the ball over 24 times and wound up losing 81–64.

Grant had a poor game overall. His totals of 6 points, 5 rebounds, and 1 assist were far below the early-season standards he had established.

Coach Krzyzewski was fuming after the embarrassing loss. "We were just totally outplayed," he said. "We played like it was our birthright to win and I hate that. So it was great that they killed us."

A long, quiet bus ride back to Durham was followed by a late-night practice session. For Grant, injury was added to the insult of the Virginia loss. During practice Antonio Lang accidentally elbowed him in the nose, breaking it. Fortunately for the Blue Devils, sophomore Thomas Hill filled in nicely for Grant during the next two games.

The Duke team had learned a valuable lesson from the Virginia loss. They played heads-up, intelligent ball and rolled through February, going 14–3. After a 79–62 win over Clemson that closed out the month, their overall record stood at 24–6. Duke had dropped only two conference road games. A hard-fought double-overtime slip at Arizona was the only other Blue Devil loss.

Duke's first outing in March was their final regular-season game. The solid team effort was highlighted by Duke's relentless defensive pressure. Guard Bobby Hurley had his best game of the season, scoring 18 points and handing out 6 assists. Center Christian Laettner also contributed 18 points to the offense. Grant gave the players defending him a run for their money, too. He drove to the hoop for massive dunks again and again, helping himself to 16 points, 5 rebounds, and 3 assists and his team to a satisfying 83–77 win over archrival University of North Carolina. The win gave them the ACC regular-season title, their first since the 1985–86 season.

A week later, in the ACC tournament championship game, they found themselves in a rematch against the UNC Tar Heels. The Blue Devils came out flat and paid for it. The Tar Heels ran them out of the building with a 96–74 thrashing. Not only was Duke embarrassed by their play, they were hurt by the players' lack of self-discipline. Now, a basketball program that had strung together four Final Four seasons in five years had just four days to turn itself around for "the big dance," the NCAA tournament. Could they do it?

Chapter Four:
1991

The Big Dance

Coach Krzyzewski reminded his players that the NCAA tournament was a brand-new season. As was the case with the Virginia loss early in the regular season, it was important for the team to learn from the UNC defeat.

Coach K's message to Grant was to play more aggressively. "Don't be afraid to make a mistake. Don't be afraid to be good." This simple advice made a lasting impression on the young player.

The Duke team entered the tournament revitalized and raring to go. The upperclassmen in particular were determined to scrub out the memory of their UNLV loss the previous year.

The Blue Devils breezed through the first four tournament games, defeating Northeast Louisiana, Iowa, Connecticut, and St. John's to win the Midwest

Regional. The closest game was a 14-point win over Connecticut.

Grant Hill, who had followed the NCAA tournament so closely growing up, was now in the middle of the action. Through four games he averaged 9.5 points, 5 rebounds, and 2.5 assists.

Next up was the rematch Coach K's squad had been looking forward to all year: Duke versus UNLV.

Nobody outside of Coach Krzyzewski himself thought the Blue Devils had a chance to win this semifinal. The Runnin' Rebels stormed into the Hoosier Dome in Indianapolis, Indiana, with a perfect 34–0 record. With their postseason games, the defending national champions had an incredible 45-game winning streak. UNLV forwards Larry Johnson and Stacey Augmon and guard Greg Anthony were all headed for the NBA. The team was being hailed as one of the greatest of all time.

In order to better prepare his team for the task at hand, Coach K made them watch the tape of the opening minutes of the embarrassing 30-point loss to UNLV. Grant could easily see how flat the Duke team had been. It reminded him of Duke's losses to Virginia and North Carolina earlier in the current season. Coach K asked his players to picture in their minds how they would play down the stretch in a close game.

The stage was set for one of the most memorable games in NCAA tournament history. From the opening tap, it was a street fight. UNLV had a reputation for being an extremely aggressive team. The Blue Devils refused to be intimidated.

Throughout the game, Grant rendered UNLV All-American forward Stacey Augmon powerless. His aggressive, blanketing "body on" style kept Augmon from getting into good shooting position. Augmon would finish with just 6 points, shooting 3 for 10 from the floor.

With just over two minutes left in the game, Duke trailed 76–71. Then Bobby Hurley sank a three-pointer, cutting the UNLV lead to 2. As UNLV inbounded the ball, the carefully honed Duke defense rose to the moment. The Runnin' Rebels and their high-powered offense were unable to take a shot. Duke got the ball back.

With time ticking out, Blue Devil sophomore forward Brian Davis threw in a layup and was fouled.

He converted the free throw for a 3-point play. Duke led 77–76.

UNLV forward Larry Johnson, the nation's most dominant player that season, hit a free throw to tie the game at 77. With 12.7 seconds remaining, Duke center Christian Laettner answered with two free throws. Now UNLV had possession, but time was on Duke's side.

UNLV inbounded the ball and instantly heaved a desperation shot toward their basket. No good!

As the buzzer sounded, the Duke players went crazy. They had beaten the unbeatable team and avenged the 1990 loss!

Duke's 79–77 upset victory over the defending national champions brought the crowd to its feet. Though he hadn't been a major offensive force in the game, Grant Hill had contributed a solid all-around performance, scoring 11 points, grabbing 5 rebounds, and dishing out 5 assists.

Coach K's most difficult task now was to temper the postgame celebration. Duke still had to face Kansas in the title game. "An ordinary team would be satisfied beating UNLV, but an ordinary team won't win on Monday," he said. But the Blue Devil players exuded confidence in their pregame comments. Even the usually quiet Grant Hill told the media he would be disappointed if Duke lost. After working so hard to return to the national championship, the Blue Devils were not planning on losing.

A crowd of more than 47,000 packed the Hoosier Dome to view the 1991 NCAA title match. Early in the game, Grant made the most memorable play of the night. Bobby Hurley shot him a precision alley-oop pass. Grant leaped, made a one-handed grab, and followed through with a thunderous jackknife dunk. The kid who had passed up open shots and deflected praise to his teammates in interviews had vaulted into the spotlight of the biggest game of all.

The power move by their freshman sensation energized the rest of the team. Not to worry, this is our night, the other Blue Devils thought. Duke had been to the Final Four nine times since 1963, but had never won the big game. They took to the court determined to make trip ten a winner.

Throughout the game they played hard, heads-up ball. The Jayhawks just couldn't keep up. Duke dominated in the second half, switching to a rarely used zone defense. Kansas was so baffled they made only one basket in the next seven minutes. With 7 minutes 47 seconds remaining in the game, Duke extended their lead to 61–47 with a series of easy layups.

Brian Davis iced the victory cake with a monumental slam dunk on a pass from Grant Hill seconds before the game ended. When the buzzer sounded, the scoreboard read 72–65. Center Christian Laettner (18 points) was named MVP. Grant finished with 10 points, 8 rebounds, and 3 assists. Guard Bobby Hurley played all eighty minutes in the semi and final, handing out 16 assists with only 6 turnovers.

After nine previous trips to the Final Four, the Blue Devils had won the first national championship in the school's history. Grant reflected on the team's accomplishment: "From Day One, it seemed we were destined to win it all. There was a special quality, a closeness, a chemistry I'd never seen on a basketball team before."

Grant Hill's final stat line of 11.2 points per game, 5.1 rebounds, 2.2 assists, 51 steals for his first college season earned him a place on the Freshman

All-American team. He also got an opportunity to play for the U.S. national team at the Pan American Games, taking home a bronze medal.

His first year at Duke had changed Grant from a quiet, somewhat shy young man to someone more open and confident. "I wish I could have it all back because I know I could have done more," he commented after the season was over. "I'm anxious for next year to start so that I can play like I know I can play right from the start."

Grant had played some of his best games against the best competition the Blue Devils faced. He scored a career-high 19 points three times versus Arizona, Michigan, and Oklahoma. His performance throughout the NCAA tournament, highlighted by his defensive effort against UNLV's Stacey Augmon (6 points) and capped off by his championship game slam dunk, was his best overall effort of the season.

With three more years to run, Grant Hill's college basketball career was looking brighter than ever.

Chapter Five:
1991–1992

The Chance to Step Forward

With the return of fellow starters Christian Laettner at center and guards Thomas Hill and Bobby Hurley, Grant Hill and the Blue Devils were primed for a big year in 1991–92. Laettner and Thomas Hill had accompanied Grant as members of the U.S. national team at the Pan Am Games. That, plus the attention surrounding Duke's national championship win, had made for a short off-season.

Coach Mike Krzyzewski knew that a tremendous amount of pressure would be placed on his team as they started the season. "Let's have fun" became the coach's three key words for success.

And fun they had! The Blue Devils stormed from the gate, winning their first 17 games. Five times Duke won by a margin of 28 or more points. Included among their wins was an 88–85 overtime thriller at Michigan versus a team of talented starters known as the Fab Five.

The Blue Devils were far and away the dominant team in the country.

Even a 2-point loss to archrival North Carolina failed to derail the Duke team. Four straight victories, including a 10-point win over Shaquille O'Neal and Louisiana State University, got the Blue Devils back on track. A 4-point conference loss at Wake Forest would be the last defeat of their banner season. They finished off with an 89–76 victory over North Carolina at Cameron Indoor Stadium.

Once again a model of consistency in the Duke precision basketball machine, Grant scored 10 or more points in each of the games during Duke's 17-game winning streak. Against Florida State he notched a career-best 26 points.

Although his presence on the court was always important, Grant became irreplaceable after Duke's first loss at North Carolina on February 5. All-American point guard Bobby Hurley, the man who directed the Blue Devils' offense on the court, broke a bone in his right foot during that game. He would be out for a month.

There was little doubt who would be expected to fill the void at point guard. Coach K called on the versatile Grant Hill to run Duke's offense.

Until then, Grant had shunned the spotlight, preferring to let his older teammates step forward. Now he knew his time had come. The responsibility would fall on his shoulders when the game was on the line. All eyes would be on him.

His first game at point guard was the matchup with Shaquille O'Neal at LSU. A national television audience watched along with a capacity crowd of almost 14,000. The intensity surrounding the game reminded Coach K and the Duke players of Final Four appearances.

Displaying his incredible versatility, Grant poured in 16 critical points from the outside. He also contributed 6 assists and 9 rebounds, and showed poise in running the team's offense throughout the entire forty-minute game.

Coach K commented on Grant's effort after the game by saying, "There were three great players out there today: Shaq, Laettner, and Hill!"

In his second game at point guard, Grant keyed a rally at Georgia Tech with a combination of outside shooting finesse and inside offensive power. His 20 points, 6 rebounds, and 5 assists were impressive, especially given the fact that he had been sick with the flu all game! Even at less than 100 percent, he played his hardest.

During his five-game stretch at the point position, Grant averaged 16.4 points, 6.2 rebounds, and 5.6 assists. The Blue Devils compiled a 4–1 record without Bobby Hurley.

Then, just when it seemed the sophomore dynamo was ready to reach even greater heights, he suffered an injury to his right ankle. Grant considered himself fortunate, though, since he missed only three games late in the regular season. The doctor's original prognosis had threatened to sideline him for the rest of the year.

With their final regular-season record an amazing 28–2, the number-one-ranked Blue Devils set out to do what no college basketball team had done since 1973: win two consecutive NCAA championships. A now-healthy starting lineup roared back in full force, taking the ACC tournament title with wins over Maryland, Georgia Tech, and North Carolina.

Their first three NCAA opponents didn't present much of a problem, either. Campbell University of North Carolina, the University of Iowa, and Seton Hall were all easily defeated. The Blue Devils were one giant step closer to their goal. But in their way stood a formidable opponent: the Wildcats of Kentucky.

Chapter Six:
1992

Back-to-Back?

The East Regional final was an epic confrontation. Throughout the first half, the Blue Devils had the lead. Center Christian Laettner was playing a heads-up game, Bobby Hurley was running the offense with precision, and the other three starters were aggressive but controlled. Then something happened.

Leading by 12 (67–55) with just over eleven minutes left in the game, Duke became uncharacteristically overconfident and eased up. Kentucky took full advantage of the situation and stormed back with a series of 3-point shots and ferocious defense. No longer an easy victory, the game went down to the final minutes.

During the last 31.5 seconds of regulation play, the lead changed hands five times. When the buzzer sounded at the end of the fourth quarter, the score was tied at 93–93. The Blue Devils and the Wildcats would fight for the win in overtime.

Each basket in the five-minute OT was a struggle. The players worked hard to give their team the lead. When Duke was behind by 3, Grant Hill ripped down a rebound and set up Bobby Hurley for a 3-point basket.

The clock ticked down the last minute of play. With 7.8 seconds left, Duke was ahead by 1. They needed only to prevent Kentucky from scoring. But Kentucky was on fire. Guard Sean Woods drove to the hoop and put up a shot. Score! Kentucky led, 103–102. Only 2.1 seconds remained.

Coach K called a time-out. Calmly, he described a play that the players all knew. However, the last time they had tried it, it had failed, costing them the game against Wake Forest late in the regular season. Would the play work this time?

It was up to Grant Hill to see that it did.

The play called for him to inbound the ball with a long pass downcourt into the hands of Christian Laettner, who would then put up a shot. In the Wake Forest game, Grant had been so tightly defended that he had thrown a bad pass. The Duke center had had to step out of bounds to catch it. He had never gotten the shot off, and the game had ended in Wake Forest's favor.

Now, with 2.1 seconds left, Grant was ready to try it again. Unlike Wake Forest, Kentucky decided to defend the passee rather than the passer. When Grant took the ball behind his own basket, no Wildcat player was in his face. But Christian Laettner was double-teamed. Grant's pass would have to make it through four wildly waving arms.

The whistle blew. Grant took the ball, reared back, and threw. It was a pinpoint perfect 75-foot pass downcourt to an open area on the foul line. Laettner raced to meet it. He scooped it up, faked left, and sank a buzzer-beating turnaround jumper!

The Duke bench erupted. A fifth straight Final Four slot had been secured by a miraculous finish!

"Fate was on our side," Grant said amid the postgame celebration. "We were destined. Even if someone had been on me, even if the pass had been off, Christian would have tipped it and it would have gone in. We still would have won somehow."

"I don't know what those things [luck and destiny] are," said a relieved Coach Krzyzewski. "I just know that the ball got put in play by our best athlete. Our best player caught it and shot it."

Though one of the most exciting games ever was behind them, the NCAA championship was still to come. In Minnesota's Metrodome for the national semifinal round, Duke faced the Indiana University Hoosiers, coached by veteran Bobby Knight. Though Duke prevented Indiana from scoring on its first 11 possessions, they struggled for the win. Yet win Duke did, 81–78.

They had earned the chance to defend their NCAA title. Their opponents were the young, brash Michigan Wolverines: the outstanding all-freshman Fab Five.

Grant was very familiar with the two most prominent members of Michigan's blue-chip squad. Wolverine forward Chris Webber and guard Jalen Rose had played against him in the national AAU tournament in St. Louis when he was in the eighth grade.

When the two teams had met in the regular season, they had been very physical. Duke had allowed a 17-point first-half lead to slip away. Only a heroic performance by Bobby Hurley — a 3-point shot and

3 straight free throws — saved the day. Duke left Michigan's Crisler Arena a narrow 88–85 winner on that December day, knowing that despite their youth this Michigan team was a legitimate championship contender.

Now the Blue Devils were ready to find out how fab the Fab Five really were.

A crowd of more than 50,000 fans flocked into the Minneapolis Metrodome. The Wolverines, known for their trash-talking aggressiveness, played a confident first half and led by 1 at intermission. Coach Krzyzewski wondered how his veteran team could be so flat in such a big game. He honestly didn't have a feel for whether his team could recover in the second half. Someone would have to step forward and take control if Duke was to have a chance.

Enter Grant Hill. The sophomore forward ignited his teammates with 6 points, 3 rebounds, a steal, and a blocked shot through one sequence. In the minutes that followed, the Blue Devils were unstoppable. They threw in 23 points to the Wolverines' 6. Duke squashed Michigan in an astounding 71–51 victory.

For the first time since 1973, college basketball had a back-to-back champion. Duke was king.

Although Bobby Hurley was named the Final Four MVP, Mike Krzyzewski was quick to point out who the key to the title game had been. Grant Hill had scored 18 points, pulled down 10 rebounds, dealt out 5 assists, blocked 2 shots, and made 3 steals in a superb all-around performance.

Michigan coach Steve Fisher praised Grant in the postgame press conference. "He's quick, he's athletic, and intelligent, and these qualities make him almost impossible to stop."

Overall Grant improved both his scoring (14) and rebounding (5.7) for the season. His free-throw accuracy showed a dramatic jump from 61 percent to 73 percent. The numbers did not escape the attention of the media. He was named United Press International second-team All-American and Associated Press honorable-mention All-American. He was also an All Final Four selection.

Though the Blue Devils would lose All-American center Laettner and steady forward Brian Davis to graduation, they would still return with a solid nucleus led by Bobby Hurley and Grant Hill the next year. Was an NCAA championship three-peat possible? The only thing for sure was that expectations for the 1992–93 team would again run high in Durham, North Carolina.

Chapter Seven:
1992–1993

"He's Really That Good"

In the spring before his junior year, Grant Hill and some other talented college players were given a once-in-a-lifetime opportunity. They were selected to help the Olympic Dream Team practice. NBA superstars Larry Bird, Michael Jordan, and Magic Johnson, who went on to lead the U.S. team to the gold medal, took the time to praise Grant's abilities.

Such a brush with stardom made Grant start to wonder whether maybe he wasn't ready to think seriously about his future career. A number of top college players had routinely been turning professional before completing their four years of school.

For a brief moment Grant considered going the pro route. But he reconsidered after consulting his father. "I'll definitely be at Duke all four years," he said in an interview with *USA Today*. "My goal when I chose Duke was to graduate."

With Christian Laettner and Brian Davis gone, Grant knew his junior season could provide more of an opportunity to be a team leader. But some questioned whether Grant was ready to assume the responsibility Coach Krzyzewski had in mind for him.

"A kid like Grant needs to be helped to get to his rightful position, to realize that he's really that good," Coach K commented about his reluctant star. "Grant being Grant, he wants to be asked to advance in the line, even when he's at the head of it."

Duke was not expected to be the powerhouse team they had been for the past two years. But they took the league by storm and breezed into January and the ACC portion of their schedule undefeated and ranked first in the nation.

An early-season highlight was a December rematch at home with Michigan. The Wolverines' Fab Five starting lineup was one year older, more mature, and looking to avenge the 20-point championship loss. For the first time since the 1991 national championship game versus UNLV, the Blue Devils entered a game as the predicted underdog.

In front of a frenzied sellout crowd of 9,314 at Cameron Indoor Stadium, Duke and Michigan played a rough defensive game. The Wolverines turned the ball over 19 times, while the Blue Devils shot just 41 percent. In the end, however, Duke prevailed, 79–68. Grant Hill played an aggressive game, contributing 15 points and 7 rebounds before he was sidelined with 4 fouls. But senior point guard Bobby Hurley was the Blue Devil standout, with 20 points, 5 assists, and only 1 turnover in a full forty minutes!

Then, on January 10, 1993, Duke tasted defeat for the first time. In a physically challenging game against Georgia Tech, Grant shot a career-high 29 points, including a monster reverse dunk and 13 straight free throws. But it wasn't quite enough. He missed a crucial free throw late in the game that cost Duke a chance to tie the score and go into overtime. An inspired Georgia Tech squad won, 80–79.

After that, Duke struggled. They barely managed to eke out a hard-earned 65–56 win against Iowa and its star big man Acie Earl. The punishing defense held Grant to 12 points. Then, the following night, Duke's 36-home-game winning streak was halted.

The Virginia Cavaliers entered Cameron Stadium looking to win their first game there since 1982. Their determination to leave victorious showed in every aspect of their game.

They played tenacious man-to-man defense, holding Duke to a mere 37 shooting percentile; Grant himself had a difficult night offensively, hitting only 6 of 16 attempts from the floor. The Cavs outrebounded the Devils as well, ripping down 50 to Duke's 37. They set the pace of the game with precision control of their half-court offense. In short, they outplayed the Devils.

Virginia left Cameron Indoor Stadium with a 77–69 triumph; for the first time since March 1990, the Blue Devils had lost on their home court.

Despite the morale-sapping defeat, the Devils bounced back to take 7 of their next 8 games, bringing their record up to 18–2. Then in mid-February, Grant's and the Blue Devils' season took a turn for the worse.

Duke was playing a close home game against Wake Forest. They would eventually lose to the Demon Deacons 98–86, but the defeat was only one of the night's catastrophes. One of their most consistent players, Grant Hill, left the game early in the second half not to return.

In practice a few weeks earlier, he had landed hard on the ball of his left foot. It was a painful injury, but not one that appeared likely to cause continued trouble. In the game against Wake Forest, however, he landed on it again — and so did other players. This time, the prognosis was bad. A fractured bone in his big toe, several more between the ball of his foot and the toe, and torn ligaments would keep him out of the lineup for the rest of the regular season.

According to Coach K, playing without Grant wasn't easy. Though the Blue Devils finished the 1992–93 regular season 24–8, they went 4–2 in their last 6 games without their versatile junior forward.

Grant returned for the first game of the ACC tournament, but his presence and 14 points didn't put Duke in the winner's circle. The two-time NCAA champs lost 69–66 to Georgia Tech.

Grant, Bobby Hurley, and the rest of their teammates had almost a week to sit and think about the NCAA tournament. The rest seemed to give them back the energy they had lost midseason. In the first round they overwhelmed 14th-seeded Southern Illinois 105–70.

But the second round proved far different. An underdog University of California–Berkeley entered the Midwest Regionals having won ten of their last eleven games. The Golden Bears couldn't wait to get their claws into the Blue Devils.

California's best player was freshman point guard Jason Kidd, who is now a member of the NBA's Dallas Mavericks. Kidd played an outstanding game, directing the California offense with calm control. But the Blue Devils weren't so easily defeated.

Bobby Hurley keyed the offense with 32 points, 9 assists, and only 1 turnover. Grant Hill, though still suffering from his injury, came through with 18 points, 7 rebounds, and 4 assists.

It wasn't enough. Though Duke led by 1 with less than 2:30 to play, the Golden Bears were not to be denied. The game was decided in the final seconds when Jason Kidd caught the ricochet off an attempted steal by Bobby Hurley. He hit a spinning shot from underneath the basket a second later, giving California a 1-point lead. Grant had fouled Kidd on the play, allowing Kidd to go to the line. Kidd sank the free throw and the Bears were up 79–77.

On Duke's next possession, Grant was called for a questionable travel. The ball went back to California, who added another 3 points to their 2-point lead. California took the game 82–77. In the span of forty short minutes, Duke's dreams of a sixth consecutive trip to the Final Four and a third straight national championship vanished.

The scene in the Duke locker room was an emotional one. Bobby Hurley and the underrated Thomas Hill had played their last games as Blue Devils. It would clearly be Grant's team the following year as a senior — if he wanted it.

Though thoughts of the pros crossed Grant's mind again, in the end he knew he had to honor his four-year commitment to Duke and its basketball program. The past year had been a warm-up for next year's leadership role.

Grant's father, Calvin Hill, was a star running back for the Dallas Cowboys.

"Baby Boy Hill" and his parents, Janet and Calvin.

Grant Hill claims playing soccer helped him develop speed. In this 1994 NCAA tournament game, he's ahead of his Purdue opponent by a step.

An excellent ball handler, Grant Hill drives to the hoop during a 1994 Final Four game versus Florida. (Duke won!)

Grant slams in two points for Duke!

In an aggressive move for the ball, Grant Hill draws a foul in a 1995 preseason Pistons game.

In flight and heading toward the hoop for two points!

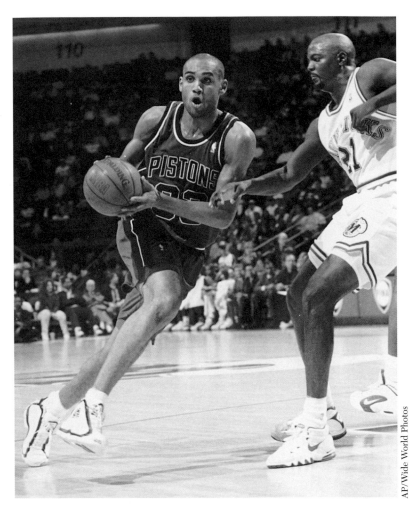

Grant makes his move.

A slam dunk by the number one vote getter in the 1995 All-Star game.

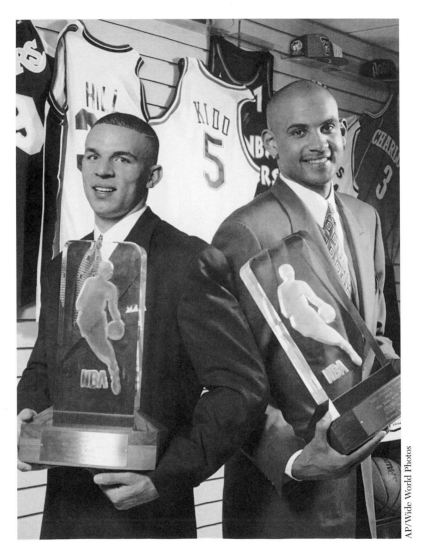

AP/Wide World Photos

Grant Hill shares 1995 Rookie of the Year award honors with Dallas Maverick Jason Kidd.

Grant Hill's Year-to-Year Statistics: College

Year	Games Played	Rebounds	Assists	Steals	Blocks	Points	Season Average	High Game
1990-1991	36	183	79	51	30	402	11.2	19
1991-1992	33	187	134	39	27	463	14.0	26
1992-1993	26	166	72	64	36	468	18.0	29
1993-1994	34	233	176	64	40	591	17.4	33

Grant Hill's Statistics: Professional

Year	Games Played	Rebounds	Assists	Steals	Blocks	Points	Season Average	High Game
1994-1995	70	445	353	124	62	1,394	19.9	33

Grant Hill's Career Highlights

1991: Member of the NCAA Championship Team
Named a Freshman All-American
Earned ACC All-Freshman honors
Named Second-Team All-ACC
Member of the USA National Team at 1991 Pan American
Games

1992: Member of the NCAA Championship Team
Named UPI Second-Team All-American
Selected as an All Final Four
Named Second-Team All-ACC
Named AP Honorable Mention All-American
Selected as Basketball Times All-Region and USBWA
All-District

1993: Named Second-Team All-American by UPI and USBWA
Named First-Team All-ACC
Winner of the Henry Iba Corinthian Award (Top Defensive
Player)
Reached 1,000-Point Mark
Member of the Olympic Development Team for the 1992
Dream Team

1994: Tri-Captain of the Duke Blue Devils
Number 33 Jersey Retired
Member of the NCAA Final Four Team
Selected as First-Team All-American
ACC Player of the Year
Named Consensus First-Team All-ACC
Named First-Team NABC All-District

1995: NBA Co-Rookie of the Year (with Jason Kidd)
Lead League Voting for NBA All-Star Team Selection
Selected to Olympic Dream Team III (for 1996 Olympics)

Chapter Eight:
1993

Off Court

Grant's junior season had been an outstanding one. He had led the team in scoring, with an average of 18 points per game. He also led the team in steals, with 64, and placed second in rebounds (6.4) and blocks (36). His performance earned him recognition in the sportswriter world: United Press International again named him a second-team All American, the Associated Press moved him up to third team, and he made the All-ACC first team. He received the highest honor for defense in college basketball, the Henry Iba Corinthian Award.

Throughout his junior year, basketball had undoubtedly been his main focus. But it wasn't the only thing in his life at Duke. Thanks to his unique upbringing as the son of a pro football player, Grant had long recognized that star athletes could use their status to raise the public's interest in community causes. The choices facing young people were of particular concern to him. He knew that his own childhood had been unusual, that not all kids were fortunate enough to have plenty of money and parents who cared about teaching the difference between right and wrong. He decided it was time to let people know he was willing to help.

During his junior year, Grant got involved with Durham's 1993 Project Graduation. The program provided a graduation party free of alcohol and drugs for students at six area high schools. As cochairperson of the program along with Duke women's tennis star Susan Sommerville, Grant had an opportunity to speak out.

"There are a lot of pressures to go and try alcohol and experiment with drugs, but I've learned that you can have a lot of fun without it," he said to the *Blue Devil Weekly*. "My father worked with the NFL's drug program, teaching about the dangers of dependency with drugs. I learned at an early stage about staying away from drugs and alcohol. Even though I'm often teased by my peers because I don't drink, it's something I believe in and stand by." To him, it just made sense to give your body all it needed to be in peak condition. You weren't hurting anyone but yourself if you did otherwise.

Keeping his own body in top form was made more challenging for Grant once basketball season was over. During the spring, he underwent foot surgery. He was on crutches for most of the summer, but when the cast came off he was able to join the eight-member USA Olympic Development team. It was a great opportunity for him to get back into basketball after a summer off, and to play with outstanding athletes he might never have had a chance to play with otherwise.

When he returned to Duke in September of 1993, he was fully recovered — and ready to assume his place at the helm of the Blue Devils.

Chapter Nine:
1993-1994

A Year of Leadership

In the 1993–94 season, the NCAA made a decision that gave Grant Hill and his teammates a terrific advantage. It involved the "closely guarded" rule, which stated that a player who was closely guarded could dribble the ball for no more than five seconds. At the start of the season, the "closely guarded" rule was eliminated.

Putting aside this rule meant a player with superior ball-handling skills could now give his offense more time to set up before he started running a play. Grant Hill had proved he was just such a player.

But despite this bright light for the Devils' offense, expectations for the 1993–94 team were lower than national championship contender. With the exception of Grant Hill, center Cherokee Parks, and forward Antonio Lang, the squad was made of mostly untested players.

Yet Grant was undaunted. In interviews with reporters, he warned that the Blue Devils were going to be "the Silent Assassins," quietly stealing victories from their opponents. "I did what any athlete in my position would do. I guaranteed a national championship," he said later.

Always known to be truthful, Grant spurred his Blue Devils to victory game after game. The scores were close, but in many instances Grant's confident leadership gave his team the edge they needed.

One game in particular stood out. On December 11, 1993, Duke triumphed over Michigan with a huge 73–63 victory. The Blue Devils' defense hounded the Wolverines the whole night. Besides pulling down 6 rebounds, Grant made a spectacular block against the Michigan center Juwan Howard that ended a Wolverine rally late in the game. "Every shot was a struggle for them and that's what we wanted it to be," Grant commented later.

Grant himself contributed to the Blue Devils' offense with 18 points, including three key 3-point shots.

Another solid road win against Iowa (79–76) high-lighted the early-season run. By mid-January, Grant Hill's prediction that Duke would reach the Final Four seemed to be coming true: The Blue Devils were the top-ranked team in the league.

A 1-point loss at home to Wake Forest failed to slow down the Blue Devils, as they efficiently reeled off 12 wins in their next 14 contests. Only their in-state rival, North Carolina, defeated them. Duke ended the season with a 28–6 record.

On Sunday, February 27, 1994, before the start of the regular season's last home game, Grant Hill had been paid the ultimate honor by the Duke University basketball program. Before the capacity crowd of more than 9,000 fans at Cameron Indoor Stadium, his jersey, number 33, took up permanent occupancy in the school's Hall of Fame. He became the eighth player to be so honored in the long, proud history of Duke basketball, joining teammates Christian Laettner (number 32) and Bobby Hurley (number 11) among the elite.

Coach K stated his feelings about the power-house threesome simply: "I hope, in however long I coach, I get to coach three kids like that again."

Grant revealed that the moment was one he had dreamed about. Janet and Calvin Hill looked on proudly as Duke president Nan Keohane presented their son with his framed jersey. Calvin, the grizzled veteran of the NFL, later said he came close to crying in front of a national television audience.

Though he too was emotional, Grant channeled his feelings in a positive direction in order to go out and win the game that followed the ceremony. His routinely brilliant 13-point, 8-rebound, 8-assist performance led the Blue Devils to a 59–47 victory against Temple. Playing thirty-nine of forty minutes, he turned the ball over only once. Defensively, he played strong, flying around the floor and blocking two shots.

Freshman guard Jeff Capel seemed to be as much in awe of the Duke senior captain as anyone watching from the stands. "He's always there giving us so much. He was telling us to play, being a great leader," Capel observed. "Sometimes it's not by word, but by example."

After the game, Grant tried to put the honor of his number's retirement in perspective. "It still really hasn't sunk in. I'm happy about the award, but I'm more happy about this team."

Duke entered the ACC tournament as the conference's regular-season champions. In the tourney opener, Grant hammered in 23 points to lead the way over Clemson. A disappointing second-round loss to Virginia (66–61) proved Grant was only human.

Though he scored 17 points and hauled in 13 rebounds, the senior captain faltered down the stretch. During second-half "crunch time," when he normally thrived, he missed two easy layups, a short jumper, and a three-pointer; he also collided with a teammate to cause a turnover and had a shot blocked. When he finally scored with seven seconds left on the clock, it was simply too little too late.

As important as Grant was to the team, Coach K and the other Blue Devils realized that they couldn't expect him to carry them alone in the NCAA tournaments. Grant himself echoed that thought. As he told each of his teammates before the NCAA tournament, "We need everybody now. Everybody has to play."

Opening at the Southeast Regional in St.

Petersburg, Florida, Duke defeated Texas Southern 82–70 in the first round with a sound team effort.

In the next game versus the Michigan State Spartans, Grant played one of the best all-around games of his career: 25 points, 5 rebounds, 7 assists, and 4 steals were only half the story; he was equally awesome on defense. He held Spartan guard Shawn Respert, who averaged 24.4 points a game, to just one shot in the first half. A jittery Respert turned the ball over eight times. Duke won by 11, 85–74.

Advancing to Knoxville, Tennessee, Grant proved himself a clutch player by taking charge down the stretch. He shot 16 of his 22 points in the second half, leading his team to a 59–49 victory over Marquette.

Duke was at the threshold of a return to the Final Four. But they weren't there yet. Standing in the doorway was an imposing foe: the Purdue Boilermakers.

Purdue was number one in the Big Ten Conference, thanks in large part to their six-foot-eight-inch forward, Glenn "Big Dog" Robinson, the NCAA's leading scorer. The Big Dog had recently sunk 44 of Purdue's 83 points in the Boilermakers' victory over Kansas.

A capacity crowd of more than 23,000 was on hand to see whether Grant Hill and the Blue Devils could handle the Big Dog and the Boilermakers.

The Duke seniors were not to be denied their chance to play in their third NCAA championship. First Grant, then Antonio Lang deprived Robinson of the ball. When the ball did get through to him, they forced him to take bad shots or routed him into a position where their center, Cherokee Parks, had a chance to block.

The aggressive defense was not without its toll. Grant wound up in early foul trouble and had to sit out. But even from the bench, his leadership skills came into play. He urged his teammates on, encouraging them to play their hardest.

His teammates responded. Guard Jeff Capel stepped forward, scoring 15 points during Grant's six-minute absence. When Grant checked back in, Duke had a 56–50 lead.

As the clock ticked off the final seconds, Duke saw that their strategy had paid off. Glenn Robinson had fouled out of the game, having scored just 12 points. Duke won an emotional 69–60 decision. Out from the shadow of Laettner and Hurley, Grant Hill was voted MVP of the regional.

The 1994 Final Four would take the Blue Devils back to the site of the ACC tournament in Charlotte, North Carolina.

The semifinal game versus the University of Florida was another Grant Hill masterpiece. His team had been struggling for much of the game. At halftime, they were down by 7. Then with 17:57 left to play in the second half, Grant Hill turned up the flame.

He hit a critical three-pointer, sparking a 25-point rally. He shut down the Gators' offensive powerhouse, Craig Brown. In one fantastic play that erased Florida's lead, Grant dribbled the full length of the court, forced Brown to back up on defense, then eased his way into the lane for a graceful turnaround jumper. The Blue Devils never looked back. From a 13-point deficit, they charged to a decisive 70–65 win.

"This could have been our last game," Grant observed. "We raised it to a new level and they couldn't stay with us." Duke was back playing for the NCAA championship for the fourth time in five years. They had shocked the experts all season. Why not one more time?

Chapter Ten:
1994

So Close . . .

There was no doubt who had led the Blue Devils to the brink of another NCAA championship. "I said I thought we could win a national championship and now we've positioned ourselves to do that," Grant said with confidence. "I feel good about that."

But being positioned to win the championship game and actually winning it were two different things. Their opponents, the Arkansas Razorbacks, had had an outstanding season. They had equal parts size, speed, and depth. They were the clear favorites going into the game.

The underdog Blue Devils fought fiercely. In the opening minutes of the second half, Duke surged ahead by 10. Then the Razorbacks followed a time-out by outscoring the Blue Devils 21–6 through the next nine minutes.

Duke's last chance to win came with less than two minutes remaining. Left alone by the defense, Grant tied the game at 70 with a three-pointer.

Then a desperation shot by Razorback forward Scotty Thurman found the net for a 3-point lead. Though Duke added 2 more points to their score, Arkansas never let up. They took the game in the end, 76–72.

In his final game as a collegian, Grant grabbed a career-high 14 rebounds, scored 12 points, and added 6 assists. Although understandably disappointed at not winning the third national championship of his college career, Grant could take pride in his season. He had led the team in scoring for the second year in a row, with 17.4 points a game, including 39 three-pointers — quite an achievement considering in his first three years combined he had attempted only 17 threes. His 5.1 assists and 1.8 steals per game were also team bests. When all the totals were added up, they showed that he was the first player in ACC history to have more than 1,900 points, 700 rebounds, 400 assists, 200 steals, and 100 blocked shots.

Grant finished as a first-team All-American and

ACC Player of the Year. Most important, his maturity, his confidence, and his ability to encourage players to work together as a team had led a young, inexperienced squad all the way to the national championship game.

At the end of his senior year in 1994, Grant donned a different kind of uniform: wearing a traditional cap and gown, he accepted his diploma, thus fulfilling his promise to graduate.

"Grant Hill is the best player I ever coached, period," Coach K said. Grant was leaving behind one of the best teams in college basketball, but another team was ready to take him in. The time to move to the NBA had finally come.

Chapter Eleven:
June 29, 1994

Draft Day

"There was no place else I wanted to play," Grant Hill once said of his NBA team, the Pistons. And after their losing season in 1994, the Detroit squad could hardly wait to get him suited up. But waiting was just what they had to do: they were third in line for draft picks.

Before their disappointing 1993–94 season, the Detroit Pistons had risen to the very pinnacle of NBA success. In 1985, coach Chuck Daly had taken the helm and built Detroit into one of the NBA's best franchises. From 1988 to 1990, players such as guard Isiah Thomas, center Bill Laimbeer, rebound specialist Dennis Rodman, sharpshooter Vinnie Johnson, and steady all-around guard Joe Dumars had led the Pistons to three straight trips to the NBA finals. Detroit had climbed to the top of the mountain with back-to-back world championships in 1989 and 1990.

Then the Pistons ball club went into a slow but steady decline. Soon after the Knicks defeated the Pistons 3 games to 2 in the 1992 playoffs, Coach Daly departed and Don Chaney stepped in. Thomas and Laimbeer left within two years of their former coach.

The Pistons slumped to sixth place in 1993–94. Coach Chaney knew something had to happen to turn his team around. Everyone involved in the decision-making process had reached the same conclusion. They needed someone who could play forward and guard with equal skill, who was intelligent and confident, and who had proved he could inspire teammates by handling himself with finesse on and off the court. In their opinion, that man was Duke University graduate Grant Hill.

Grant had come to Detroit with his father a few weeks before draft day. He met with the Pistons' owner, Bill Davidson, as well as Billy McKinney, vice president in charge of operations, and Chaney. He impressed everyone.

As McKinney stated after meeting with Grant,

"He spoke so well, listened well, and knew so much about the history of our organization. It was like he studied up on us."

Grant also met with guard Joe Dumars, the lone remaining Piston from Detroit's championship seasons. Over dinner, Dumars got an up-close and personal look at the potential first-round draft choice. He agreed with the rest of the Pistons organization: This kid was a very special person. Dumars couldn't help noticing how respectful and polite Grant was.

Assistant coach K. C. Jones summed up the Pistons' reactions in one statement: "Grant's a winner."

All that stood in the Pistons' way were the teams that had the first and second draft picks. Predraft speculation had the Milwaukee Bucks taking Purdue University's Glenn "Big Dog" Robinson in the first round. Then the Dallas Mavericks were sure to pick the University of California's Jason Kidd, basketball insiders thought. But there was no guarantee that this would be one of those occasions when everything went according to plan.

June 29, 1994, NBA draft day, finally arrived. The

Milwaukee Bucks did in fact make Purdue's Robinson the first overall pick. The Mavericks then stepped up. Coach Don Chaney tried unsuccessfully to prepare himself for the possibility of not getting Grant Hill.

"I was breathing erratically and I literally held my breath when the Mavericks were making their pick," he told one reporter later.

As expected, the Mavericks chose Jason Kidd. Both Coach Chaney and Billy McKinney breathed a tremendous sigh of relief. Finally, they thought, the Pistons had gotten the break they needed. Without further delay, they used their third-round draft pick to add Grant Hill to the Pistons roster.

The club wasted no time in bringing their newest player to Detroit to meet the press. Less than twenty-four hours after his draft selection, Grant Hill was holding a Detroit Pistons jersey, bearing his old Duke number, 33, over his gray business suit at his new home court, the Palace of Auburn Hills.

When he saw the large media turnout, Grant seemed surprised. "I thought there would just be four or five people here; I'm glad you all came out," he observed. "This is great; it still feels like a dream.

Maybe I should pinch myself . . . well, maybe I shouldn't or I might wake up."

Billy McKinney couldn't have been more pleased.

"I had a little formula," he said, referring to the type of player he and the rest of the Detroit organization were looking for. "TCTP: talent, character, and a team player. This particular player embodies that phrase."

Grant was as happy to be a Detroit Piston as the Pistons were to have him. A congratulatory call from President Bill Clinton added to his excitement. Accompanied by his dad and his recently acquired agent, Lon Babby, Grant concluded his first meeting with the press with some encouraging words that extended beyond basketball to the local community. "To me, Detroit represents everything good in professional sports. They've got good players and good fans. I think it's a good fit."

Chapter Twelve:
September 22, 1994

The Deal

Even before he had signed a contract with the club, twenty-one-year-old Grant Hill set out to make a positive impact on his new community.

The city of Detroit has struggled with a number of problems common to many urban centers throughout America. As Grant looked around his adopted hometown, he decided he would do all he could to make a difference.

Almost two months before actually putting the Pistons jersey on for the first time, Grant, in conjunction with Fila, a sportswear and footwear company, donated $120,000 to citywide recreation projects. He formed the Grant Hill Summer Basketball program, which in its first eighteen months of operation benefited more than 1,800 boys and girls who live in inner-city Detroit.

At a repaving of a basketball court in the city's Belle Isle park, Grant appeared with his mother and father before a crowd of young fans. The Pistons' number one draft choice expressed his thoughts on the occasion.

"Through this program we can excite the children of Detroit about academic achievement while helping them improve their basketball skills," he said. The academic benefits he referred to included workshops and tutoring for the youngsters. Today, the free ten-week-long program has set an example for the entire country.

Grant's parents could not have been prouder of their son. Calvin Hill talked about his ability to create a "sharing experience." Janet Hill wanted to make certain that everyone knew it was all Grant's idea to do "something meaningful before he started playing" in Detroit.

The words of Grant's agent, Lon Babby, summed up the meaning of the young athlete's gesture. "He's going to be special for this city, the NBA, and for the Pistons."

"I think it's neat being a role model," Grant said. "You can't ask for anything more than to be put in a position to have a positive effect on young people." Hill's words were definitely a breath of fresh air to the beleaguered sports world. His feelings were in direct opposition to those of veteran NBA superstar Charles Barkley, a forward with the Phoenix Suns. Barkley had made it clear that he did not consider himself a role model at all.

Perhaps thirteen-year-old Eric Talley, one of the many children who benefited from Grant Hill's city recreation program, said it best. "Most of these NBA people just want to live the glamorous life and chill in their mansions, but he's taking out time to be here with us and trying to help."

Grant's attitude toward living the "glamorous life" was clearly demonstrated when it came to negotiating his first professional contract. The process was unlike those involving the majority of athletes today.

"I pretty much want whatever is fair," he stated. "That's all I want." This was a sharp contrast to Glenn "Big Dog" Robinson, one of the two players drafted ahead of him. Robinson demanded a $100 million multiyear deal from the Milwaukee Bucks. It was simply not Hill's style to place himself in the same salary range or to bring attention to himself by insisting on such an enormous sum.

He had made it clear to the Pistons management that he had no desire to hold up the contract procedure by playing hard to get. He wanted to report to training camp and begin to work out with the team on time. As a result, contract negotiations progressed much more smoothly than is normally the case with NBA first-round draft choices. By mid-September, Grant Hill's first professional contract was wrapped up.

On September 22, 1994, the deal was announced at a huge press conference. Like many professional contracts, Hill's eight-year, $45 million pact included a number of incentive bonuses. But unlike so many other agreements, the bonuses would be earned based on the *team's* achievements, not his own. In a clear demonstration of his hopes for making a difference to the Pistons, Hill agreed that Detroit would have to make the playoffs and increase their overall winning percentage before he would be paid the incentives.

The contract signing went off without a hitch.

Grant Hill was now truly a member of the Pistons basketball family.

"He's my favorite player!" Detroit coach Don Chaney exclaimed. "Unselfish, sound fundamentally, along with being big and versatile." Assistant coach K. C. Jones noted that Grant was a "worker and intelligent." Vice president Billy McKinney could barely control his emotions. "I'm elated. Being able to have him from the start of training camp was an essential to help in his early development as a player."

All summer, Grant had been working out at Duke with a large group of current pros and former college players. Yet despite his intense preparation, the former Blue Devil was somewhat overwhelmed and a little nervous about the upcoming training camp.

How would he stack up against the pros?

Chapter Thirteen:
October 7, 1994

Training Camp

On October 7, 1994, training camp opened at the Palace of Auburn Hills. The first week of practice was closed to both the public and the media. Five days into camp, Detroit held an intrasquad scrimmage.

Guard Joe Dumars, who was the team captain, a five-time NBA All-Star, and MVP of the 1989 NBA finals, excitedly described the blue-chip rookie's first week. "Grant is so explosive to the basket," he said. "He has such great body control. In our first practice he went to make a move on me. He went right by me to the hoop. Only one guy has done that to me, and his name is Michael Jordan."

It was the first of many times Grant Hill would be compared to Michael Jordan. Like Jordan, Grant offered his team a complete package of shooting, passing, rebounding, and ball-handling skills. On top of that, he proved his nice-guy image was not just a front he put on for the media. On court and off, that was just who he was.

Grant accepted the typical professional sports "rookie treatment" with good humor. He got coffee and did errands for the Pistons' veteran players. He understood it was all part of paying dues. "The good thing is next year I'll get to mess with a rookie," he jokingly told *Sports Illustrated for Kids.*

Grant's closest friend on the team was captain Joe Dumars. A ten-year veteran of the NBA, Joe was a good source of information regarding life in the pros. It was important to Grant to be as educated as possible about what to expect in his new league; Joe did what he could to help the rookie learn.

Following an intensive week of training camp, the Pistons were ready for their first exhibition game. Detroit sports fans were eagerly anticipating the debut of the most important athlete in town since running back Barry Sanders had joined the Detroit Lions several years earlier.

"I wouldn't want anyone to be upset with my first game," Grant said with a smile the day before taking the court for the first time. "I'm excited for the first game. Joe might have to calm me down just like last week (at the first practice)."

The New Jersey Nets were the Pistons' opponents in their preseason opener. The crowd at the Palace buzzed about their new prize player. By the end of the game, the buzz had become a roar.

It took just five seconds for Grant Hill to get his name on the scoresheet. Off the opening tap, he literally flew to a pass from Joe Dumars, grabbing it for an alley-oop easy layup. "He's the real thing," the Pistons captain commented later. "Grant's court sense is extraordinary."

Playing 32 of 48 minutes, Grant scored 22 points, including 12 of 14 from the free-throw line, grabbed 4 rebounds, handed out 4 assists, and plucked 4 steals in the 123–117 victory. His fluid grace made the game look effortless.

The Michael Jordan comparisons began pouring in. Other observers compared him to one of his own personal heroes, Julius "Dr. J" Erving, who had revolutionized the game a generation earlier with his dunks and hang-in-the-air technique. Still others said he was the next Larry Bird or Magic Johnson.

Coach Don Chaney was optimistic about his team during the preseason, commenting that they always appeared eager to practice and that they got along well.

Grant summed up his own feelings about the team: "The day I was drafted, I looked at the roster and thought, 'Playoffs.' After the first day of training camp I thought the same thing." Although they may still have been a long way from championship level, the Pistons had hopes for the future in the person of number 33.

Chapter Fourteen:
November 4, 1994

Rookie Year Begins!

"I'm ready to attack," Grant Hill told the *Detroit Free Press* on the eve of his first NBA campaign.

He knew that an NBA game would be a whole different experience from his college games. Respect on the court would have to be earned. But the self-confidence he had developed through his sensational four-year college career would prove invaluable.

Grant wasted no time making an impact in the NBA. A capacity crowd of more than 21,000 filled the Palace on November 4, 1994, ready to witness his regular-season debut.

They were not disappointed. Although the Pistons would drop their home opener to the Los Angeles Lakers 115–98, Grant would lead his team in scoring with 25 points, including a 3-point play in the third quarter that cut the Lakers' lead to 3 and a two-handed slam dunk over the night's top scorer, Laker Nick Van Exel. He also contributed 10 rebounds, 5 assists, and 3 blocked shots.

"Grant is going to be a Hall of Fame player. He is spectacular," observed Laker coach Del Harris.

Grant appreciated the compliment, but inwardly vowed to work even harder to help his new team to victory. The following night, with his parents in attendance, Detroit bounced back with a 114–109 overtime win at Atlanta.

The Pistons, winners of only twenty games the previous year, burst from the gate with a surprising five wins in their first eight outings. Grant Hill led the Pistons in scoring six times, matching his opening-game high of 25 in a game against the Charlotte Hornets.

His impact as a rookie was undeniable, yet some felt he was being expected to achieve the impossible. "I'd like to see him grow and become Grant Hill and not Michael Jordan," Coach Chaney pointed out early in his young star's rookie season. "Everyone's putting him up on a pedestal. It adds more pressure. He has to live up to a reputation that he hasn't even developed yet."

In general, Grant seemed to be surprised by his early success. "I never thought it would be like this; I thought I'd be struggling to make the starting lineup."

His considerable talents weren't the only things about him being noticed. In an era when many athletes taunt, complain, and otherwise put down their sport, Grant continued to conduct himself as a gentleman both on and off the court. As Coach Chaney said, "He brings good things to this game. He's a good guy, with a great work ethic."

The reputations of other star players couldn't help but pale in comparison. One man in particular fell short: Glenn "Big Dog" Robinson.

In the public's eye, the two rookie small forwards were exact opposites. While Grant had negotiated his contract quickly and smoothly, Robinson had held out for more money. Where Grant was open and personable, Robinson let his agent do the talking. In the end, Grant was seen as the good guy and Robinson the bad guy.

Since Grant considered Robinson a friend, it was a comparison that he had never liked. But the media ran with it. So when the first matchup between the two players came on November 23, 1994 — Thanksgiving Eve — the public couldn't wait to see which man would come out on top.

Big Dog Robinson had led the nation in scoring at Purdue the previous year, averaging 30.3 points a game. His season low of 12 points had come in the NCAA Southeast Regional final, in a game against Duke when he had been guarded by Grant Hill. It had been one of Grant's best defensive games in his college career — and a performance he was to repeat that night at the Palace.

The Big Dog hit just 2 of 14 attempts from the floor. He turned the ball over 6 times, including once when a double-team effort by Grant Hill and Johnny Dawkins forced him to travel. Robinson was so frustrated by that turnover that he slammed the ball to the floor in anger. He finished the game with only 9 points.

Grant, on the other hand, chalked up 20 points. In one spectacular play, he flew over Milwaukee's Lee Mayberry, rolled the ball into the bucket and drew the foul, then added a free throw to convert

2 points into 3. On top of that, he added 6 rebounds and 7 assists. The Pistons prevailed, 113–108.

The next day, Grant got up extra early to deliver Thanksgiving meals to housebound senior citizens.

Chapter Fifteen:
1994-1995

Midseason Changes

Through ten games Grant was averaging 20.7 points (51.1 shooting percentage) and playing more than thirty-eight minutes a game. The win over Milwaukee was hardly a classic game, but it did allow Detroit to take an up-close look at one of the two players selected ahead of Grant Hill in the draft.

The Pistons completed the season's opening month with a 7–6 record. While not stellar, it was encouraging for a team that had lost more than three quarters of their games the previous year. Grant's first-month averages — 19.5 points, 5.1 rebounds, and 4.5 assists — were good enough for him to be named the NBA's Rookie of the Month. His shooting percentage from the floor was a shade below 50 (49.5), but from the free-throw line Grant shot an impressive 82.6 percent.

He was the team leader in assists; he stood second in scoring and fourth in rebounding. He had been the Pistons' scoring leader in seven games and had chalked up 20 or more points eight times.

Grant's two top all-around performances had been in a pair of Detroit wins at the Palace. On November 8 versus the Minnesota Timberwolves, he had scored 22 points, including an alley-oop dunk worthy of news highlight film. He also dished out 8 assists. On November 27, he had tied veteran guard Joe Dumars for scoring honors with 21 points, along with 8 assists and a team-leading 6 steals.

Game after game, the six-foot-eight-inch forward displayed his astonishing versatility. Don Chaney spoke for the entire Detroit organization when he said, "We knew he would be a great player in the NBA, but we didn't think he would be this good this early."

Veteran NBA observers spoke of Grant's "court awareness," his ability to know everything that was going on around him during the game. Others were more impressed with his "first step," the explosive initial move that allowed "the Gentleman Slam Dunker," as *Sports Illustrated* once called him, to beat defenders to the basket time and again. And still others raved about his defensive ability.

As effortless as Grant's game might have looked, hard work was still the major contributor to his success. The work ethic passed on from his parents and developed under Coach K at Duke did not disappear. After shooting a dismal 3 for 13 versus the Miami Heat, Grant was on the court tossing in 200 jump shots after practice the next day.

As a team, the Pistons were performing much better overall. The outstanding play of guard Joe Dumars, a perennial All-Star, was a given. Forward Terry Mills was improving. And the newcomers at center, Oliver Miller and Mark West, had seriously upgraded a problem area. But it was the rookie who had the greatest impact on Detroit's successful start.

The Pistons' visits to cities around the NBA took on the shape of concert tours. Grant was becoming an incredible magnet for both media and fans. He handled the attention with his usual grace, commenting only that he hoped it wasn't a bother to his teammates. After all, Grant could understand the fans' attitudes toward seeing him. He himself had to face his heroes every game he played!

"You're playing against guys you grew up idolizing," he said. "Before the game, you're sort of in awe. But once you get on the court, you forget who they are, and you work to beat them."

Unfortunately, the euphoria felt in November during Grant's NBA Rookie of the Month performance was erased as the NBA season moved into its second month.

December turned out to be a dismal 2-win, 11-loss showing for the Pistons. Illness was part of the problem. On one awful night, later called Black Friday, both Grant and Joe Dumars suffered a severe bout of the flu; Grant was sent home before the game against the Chicago Bulls even started. That same night, point guard Lindsey Hunter broke his ankle.

The hectic pace and pressures of the NBA were catching up to Grant. His game slumped; a 21-point effort in a losing cause versus the Charlotte Hornets would be his best offensive game.

Despite his rocky second month, Grant had earned the admiration of fellow players. "He's got my vote for Rookie of the Year," said NBA superstar Charles Barkley, after the Pistons defeated the

Suns. Grant took the scoring lead among the NBA's other rookies, with an average of 20.1 points a game.

In fact, there was only one area in which his game suffered night after night. As opposing teams became more familiar with his style, they began to control his inside offensive moves.

It was in a December game against the Indiana Pacers in Indianapolis that Grant felt the full force of this control. Pacers guard Derrick McKey showed him just how tough defense in the NBA could be. He allowed Grant to take 12 shots, but all were from the outside. Only 4 went in. Though Grant contributed with 7 rebounds, 4 steals, and 3 assists, his point total and shooting percentage were well below his average of 20 points and 50 percent.

The game was a valuable learning experience. Most of his points so far had been from dunks and drives to the basket. Now that avenue was being closed off. That left the outside jump shot, which until now he hadn't proved he could hit consistently.

Grant suddenly had to work extra hard to improve his weakest area. "It's something I need to do," he admitted. "I feel confident in taking jump shots, even though they don't always go in."

As the new year arrived, Grant Hill was hopeful his game and the Pistons' record would improve. But it wasn't to be. The setbacks that had plagued them in December continued in January. Mark Macon and Oliver Miller were sidelined with injuries, then Grant himself was diagnosed as having a condition called plantar fascilitis, an inflammation of the sheath that protects the sole of the foot. The condition is common to athletes whose sport involves a lot of running. Pistons captain Joe Dumars was hobbled by the same injury.

"So many of us were hurt that we began to compete over the street clothes we wore on the bench," Grant recalled.

Through the first two months of his NBA career, Grant had already played twenty-six games, virtually an entire college schedule. There were still almost four full months to go in the regular season. Getting accustomed to the grind of the pro calendar is often a difficult experience for NBA rookies. Grant proved to be no exception. On top of the foot injury, he found he was often exhausted at the end of a road trip. Things were better when they played at home, but he still had trouble falling asleep quickly.

Despite being run down and in pain, Grant wanted to play. He received a medical okay in mid-January. On January 28, he returned to the lineup to stay.

Teammates and fans alike warmly welcomed him back. In an exciting 89–85 win over Miami, he scored 14 points and contributed 8 rebounds and 3 assists. In a game versus the Los Angeles Clippers at the end of the month, he had one of his best nights of the season, scoring a team-high 27 points.

Grant Hill now had three months of NBA play under his belt. He had met the challenges head on — now he was about to reap one of the rewards.

Chapter Sixteen:
February 12, 1995

All-Star!

The end of January signaled the midseason mark, the time when fans voted for the players they wanted to see in the NBA All-Star game. When the ballots for this game were tabulated, the results were staggering. Grant Hill had earned 1,289,585 votes, more than any other player, including Michael Jordan! It was the first time a rookie had ever led the voting, and it spoke volumes about his popularity and the excitement his skill had inspired.

On the day the vote was officially announced, Grant's stat line read this way: 17.9 points a game, 4.9 rebounds, 4.2 assists, 1.9 steals, and 1 block.

The overall numbers would have been impressive for any NBA player, let alone a rookie just three months into his professional career. But the numbers alone didn't account for the tremendous support from the fans.

Many people felt the recent departures of Magic Johnson, Michael Jordan (both of whom later returned to basketball), and Larry Bird, not to mention Detroit's own Isiah Thomas, had sapped the NBA of some of its most charismatic players. A new style had taken over: trash-talking, self-promoting players perhaps best epitomized by the flashy Dennis Rodman.

The message sent by the All-Star voters was loud and clear: Fans were tiring of this new attitude. They were ready for a class act to revitalize their faith in the NBA.

Grant couldn't help responding to the overwhelming public reaction. "You like to think they vote for you because of pure talent," he told the *Detroit Free Press*, "but I know it's not just that."

The best guess on the incredible voting numbers posted by Grant — some 25,000 more than the second-place finisher, Orlando Magic center Shaquille O'Neal — is that fans responded to him for many reasons. His combination of an on-and-off-court grace and class had, sadly, become a rare sight.

On February 12, Grant and fellow Piston Joe Dumars took their places next to Shaquille O'Neal, forward Scottie Pippen of the Chicago Bulls, and guards Anfernee Hardaway of the Orlando Magic and Reggie Miller of the Indiana Pacers in the Eastern Conference's All-Star starting lineup.

In honor of his father, Grant decided to wear the number 35 instead of his regular number 33. Calvin Hill had worn number 35 throughout his thirteen-year NFL career.

Before an estimated worldwide television audience of 550 million viewers, the stage was set for the 1995 NBA All-Star game. When the players were introduced before the game, the deafening roar from the crowd that followed "Grant Hill" left no doubt as to who the people's choice was.

Though the final score of the game, West 139–East 112, was a disappointment to Detroit fans, Grant's performance proved he deserved the votes he had received. Overall he played twenty minutes and collected 10 points, 3 assists, and 2 steals. His shooting percentage from the floor (5 of 8) far outweighed a disappointing performance from the free-throw line, where he missed all 4 attempts. Veteran Dumars did his part to settle his young teammate by setting Grant up for three of his five baskets, three straight late in the first half. Twice Grant converted alley-oop passes from Dumars and Anfernee Hardaway into spectacular two-handed dunks.

"I was so nervous being on the court with these guys," he said. "I guess it was more nervous energy, because I got a little tired. It was fun. It feels good. I'm a little more confident in myself, although I didn't play great. I think it will carry over for the rest of the season."

After the All-Star game, Grant was in demand more than ever. In fact, it had become apparent that one word missing from his considerable vocabulary was "no." Interviews, TV appearances, and the running of his new business, GranHCo., were taking up what little spare time he had.

At home, a local bookstore had become about the only place he could go in public. On the road, he had to check into hotels under aliases and stay in his room except for games, practices, and interviews. Nobody in the history of the National

Basketball Association, perhaps in all of sports, had become so big a celebrity in such a short period of time.

Even his fan mail was overwhelming. When the more than 150 letters a day got too much for the Pistons' media staff to handle, Grant took stock of his situation.

"I guess I need to find a way to please people and still please myself a little," he observed to the *Detroit Free Press.* "This is all new to me. I'm still learning as I go." He decided it was time to concentrate even more on becoming the player the Pistons needed to improve their 17–29 record.

Chapter Seventeen:
February and March 1995

A Disappointing Second Half

The Pistons' first game after the All-Star break was with the New York Knicks, one of the league's top contenders, guided by the expertise of former Laker coach Pat Riley. They were making their first visit of the season to the Palace.

"I always liked his game," New York's All-Star center Patrick Ewing said in reference to Grant. "I always felt he had the ability to be the next Scottie Pippen or Michael Jordan."

With his foot problem finally cleared up and the All-Star game behind him, Grant was raring to go. His performance in the Knicks game was one of his best of the year.

He got off to a slow start, missing his first 3 shots. Then something clicked. He hit an incredible 11 buckets in a row, only 2 shy of the team record set by Isiah Thomas! With his characteristic explosive first step, he dribbled circles around his defender time and again. His 25 points, 8 assists, and 3 steals led the Pistons on the stat sheet. Detroit defeated New York 106–94; Grant outshot Ewing by 1 point for game-high honors.

The Pistons would win just twice more in February, ending the month with a 20–34 record. Grant continued to play well; even when his shooting was off, he balanced his weakness by contributing in other areas. For example, in a game against San Antonio where he went 4 for 13, he came up with a season high of 11 assists.

The month of March began on a winning note for both the Pistons and Grant Hill. He threw in 24 points to lead the Pistons to a 92–79 win over the Pacers. Then, a 9-assist effort combined with Joe Dumars's 19 points resulted in a solid road win of 98–91 over Jason Kidd's Mavericks. After a loss at Cleveland, Grant demonstrated his versatility by contributing 25 points, 9 rebounds, 7 assists, and 5 steals in a win at Washington. It was his most complete performance of the season.

Then the momentum died. The Pistons lost their

next six in a row. Late in March, their record a dismal 23–42, the Pistons had only one thing to keep their fans happy: Grant Hill. By this point in the season, most people were speaking his name in conjunction with the Rookie of the Year award.

Chapter Eighteen:
April 1995

Rookie Extraordinaire

The candidates for the NBA Rookie of the Year award were familiar. Glenn "Big Dog" Robinson of the Milwaukee Bucks was having a solid first season. Dallas Mavericks point guard Jason Kidd had had an immediate impact on his team with his expert passing skills. And Grant Hill, who had been chosen third in the draft after Robinson and Kidd, was enjoying an outstanding debut despite his team's losing record.

As the buzz about Rookie of the Year got louder, the consensus seemed to be that Glenn Robinson was not in the running after all. In many people's minds, the fact that he had held out so long before agreeing to a contract, missing much of training camp in the process, had hurt his conditioning and smooth adjustment to the NBA. In the end, he simply wasn't a solid, all-around player.

Meanwhile, the competition between Grant Hill and the former University of California–Berkeley star turned Maverick, Jason Kidd, was heating up. Whenever the two rookies met on the court, people paid close attention to how they played. In a matchup against the Mavericks in early March, Grant had barely missed the Pistons' first triple-double since 1987 — his 15 points, 9 rebounds, and 9 assists in thirty-eight minutes left him 1 shy in rebounds and assists. Meanwhile, Jason Kidd had become the third guard in NBA history to be named Player of the Week. The other two had been Magic Johnson in 1980 and Michael Jordan in 1985.

Usually quiet, Grant let his feelings about the competition be known.

"Being Rookie of the Year is a goal of mine. It's something I want to get. It's now or never."

The race for Rookie of the Year promised to be close. But before the winner could be announced, the remaining two months of the season had to be played. In mid-March, fans got a chance to compare the two contenders side by side again.

The Mavericks rode into town with a 3–1 record at the same time Jason Kidd was honored as Player of the Week by the NBA. Kidd had followed up his 20-point, 10.5-assist-average week by contributing 20 points (8 of 16 shooting), 5 rebounds, 9 assists, 5 steals, and 2 blocks in a 102–100 overtime victory over Cleveland.

Grant hit a career-high 32 points, but it was Jason Kidd who left the Palace smiling. The Mavericks emerged winners, 102–94.

A quick look at the contenders' stats for the game shows how their skills compared: Jason Kidd played 31 minutes, shot 6 for 12 including one three-pointer, pulled down 3 rebounds, and keyed 7 assists. He ended the night with 15 points. Grant Hill played 42 minutes, shot 12 for 25, and contributed 9 rebounds and 4 assists. He was 8 for 10 from the free-throw line, ending with 32 points.

Two nights later, the Boston Celtics visited the Detroit suburbs. In front of a sellout crowd of 21,454, Grant played his most dominating all-around game of the season. He led the Pistons in every major statistical category as Detroit nipped Boston, 104–103.

Grant's 33 points were a career high. In addition, he grabbed a season-best 16 rebounds. His 8 assists and 3 steals were also team highs for the evening. And again he had outscored one of the game's all-time great players, Dominique Wilkins. It was truly a memorable night for the NBA's aspiring Rookie of the Year.

The young and inconsistent Pistons followed up the victory over Boston by dropping their final two March contests to San Antonio and New York. Grant again asserted himself, leading the team in rebounds and assists in both games. But overall the Pistons' 4–11 mark was a disappointment, especially to the former Blue Devil, who had been accustomed to winning his biggest games in late March.

With a record of 25 wins and 45 losses, it certainly looked as if April would be the final month of basketball for the Detroit Pistons. Coach Don Chaney had made progress rebuilding the once proud franchise, but everyone knew the playoffs were out of reach.

In the first game of the month at home versus Washington, Grant matched his career high by pouring in 33 points in a 110–105 win. On the road in Orlando, the Pistons dropped a game to the brash title contenders by a mere 3 points. Hosting the

Magic two nights later, the Pistons avenged the loss with a 104–94 victory in front of a sold-out house.

Grant had his first triple-double statistical performance in this crowd-pleasing match. The seeming ease with which he earned his 23 points, 11 rebounds, and 10 assists at least left his fans feeling there was hope for the next season.

Disappointment followed this achievement, however. Once again Detroit wallowed in a lengthy losing streak, dropping five straight, including a 129–104 defeat in Boston. The one shining star was Grant, who led the scoring with 31 points.

Then, hosting Cleveland at the Palace, the Pistons won their final home game of the year. The 85–76 defeat of the Cavaliers saw a game-high 26-point effort from Grant Hill.

Losses to Chicago, Atlanta, and Miami closed out the year on a down note. Though Grant equaled his season-best 33 points for a third time in the game against Atlanta, it wasn't enough to pull a win from the dejected team. The season was over.

Chapter Nineteen:
May 17, 1995

Kidd Versus Hill

There was no denying that Grant Hill had had a terrific rookie season. As the experts acknowledged, the Class of 1994 was one of the NBA's finest ever. Grant received first-team All-Rookie honors. He also became the first Pistons player since 1981–82 to score 1,000 or more points in his rookie year, finishing with 1,394 points — the team high for the season — in spite of the fact that he had been sidelined for twelve games! The total placed him third on the Pistons' all-time rookie scoring list behind Kelly Tripucka's 1,772 in 1981–82 and Dave Bing's 1,601 in 1966–67.

Grant's 19.9 average points per game placed him a solid 20th in the league overall. Consistency on offense had already become his trademark. He had scored 20 or more points in 38 of 70 games, and in double figures a reliable 65 of 70 games, including the last 26 in a row. Although the midseason foot injury had cost him a dozen games, he had still averaged 38.3 minutes a game for a rank of 8th in the NBA. His quickness on defense was exemplified by his 1.77 average of steals per game, 12th place in the league.

With the season over, the only question remaining in the minds of Piston fans was who the Rookie of the Year would be. As always, the balloting was to be handled by sportswriters and broadcasters. While both Jason Kidd's and Grant Hill's stats spoke volumes — Kidd had helped the Mavericks to 23 more victories than the previous season's, with impressive stats of 11.7 points, 5.4 rebounds, 7.7 assists, and 1.91 steals — many felt the fact that the Pistons had lost 30 games by 10 or more points would damage Grant's chances.

On May 17 the vote was in. As predicted, it was a dead-heat race. Each player had received 43 of a possible 105 votes! In the final analysis, it had been impossible to separate the two first-year phenoms. Kidd was a key player who had helped his team improve dramatically. The Mavericks guard was also the only rookie to finish in the top ten in two major statistical categories. But Grant's accomplishments couldn't be denied.

So, for the first time in twenty-four years, the Rookie of the Year award would be shared.

As expected, Grant reacted with characteristic humility. "I don't mind sharing this award with Jason at all. It's an honor, and it makes up a little for not being in the playoffs. This was something I was shooting for. Now my dad will have to move his Rookie of the Year [1969 Offensive Rookie of the Year, NFL] out of the way."

But Grant was not about to rest on his laurels. He was looking forward to the challenges of the next season. He stated his goals in no uncertain terms: "My dad also has his Super Bowl ring [1971 with the Dallas Cowboys]," he said with a smile. "I'll have to get one to shut him up."

Grant Hill, NFL star Calvin Hill's six-foot-eight-inch, 225-pound son, league-high All-Star vote recipient, and co–Rookie of the Year, continues to make an impact on the basketball world as well as the general public. Through his company, GranHCo., he's signed deals with Sprite, Fila, and

Kellogg's, among other companies. He published his autobiography, *Grant Hill: Change the Game,* in early 1996; all proceeds from the book are being given to children's and education-based charities. The future stretches before him, illuminated by his own quiet ambition and amazing ability.

"I'm not a rookie anymore," he said on the last page of his book. "The difference between now and last year is that I am a year wiser. I don't expect to make rookie mistakes. If you're smart, you learn from your failure. I like to think I'm smart. I like to think I learned a lot from last season."

Grant Hill continued to shine into the 1995–96 season. As of the All-Star break, he led the Pistons in all three major statistical categories: points (21.3), rebounds (9), and assists (6.4). Though the Pistons continue to struggle as a team, their future is surely looking up, thanks to their youngest star.

Matt Christopher

Sports Bio Bookshelf

Michael Jordan

Steve Young

Wayne Gretzky

Grant Hill

All available in paperback from Little, Brown and Company

Join the Matt Christopher Fan Club!

To become an official member of the Matt Christopher Fan Club,
send a business-size (9½" x 4") self-addressed stamped envelope
and $1.00 (in cash or a check payable to Little, Brown) to:

Matt Christopher Fan Club
℅ Little, Brown and Company
34 Beacon Street
Boston, MA 02108